Copyright © 2017 Thomishia Booker

ISBN-13: 978-0-578-41633-5

This book is sold subject to the condition that it shall not, by way of trade or otherwise, be lent, resold, hired out or otherwise circulated without the publisher's prior consent in any form of binding or cover other than that in which it is published and without a similar condition including this condition being imposed on the subsequent publisher.
The moral right of the author has been asserted.

Illustrations Copyright © Thomishia Booker

Book Design by Cassandra Bowen, Uzuri Designs
http://uzuridesignsbooks.com

My Brown Skin

Thomishia Booker

Illustrated by Jessica Gibson

My skin is the perfect shade of brown,

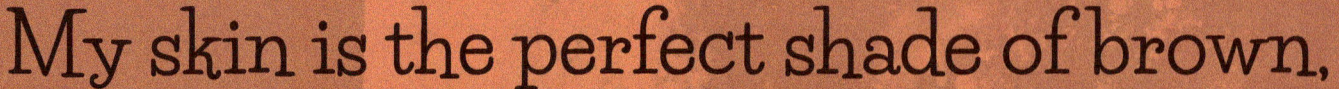

I love it so much,
　　　　I want to tell everyone around.

When I walk outside you will notice my skin glows,

From my head, to my fingers, to my shoulders, to my toes.

Brown is the color of the earth and the roots of a tree,

My skin is brown and perfect just like my mommy's.

Brown is the color of my favorite teddy bear who loves to eat honey.

My skin color means strength and power,

The color of kings sitting in the highest tower.

Did I tell you brown is my favorite color?
It reminds me of my granny's warm apple pie sprinkled with brown sugar.

My skin color is unique, it's one of a kind,

When God created me I was the only thing on his mind.

My skin is brown which means love,
My skin is sun-kissed from
the heavens above.

When I look in the mirror I see my little brown nose,

I love my brown skin and it shows!

Dedicated to Carter.
I love you to the
moon and back.
Always love who you
are because you are
enough!

S.W.A.K

CPSIA information can be obtained
at www.ICGtesting.com
Printed in the USA
LVHW071716160719
624279LV00019B/566/P